One Bad Man

AMY LAURENS

OTHER WORKS

Find other works by the author at
www.amylaurens.com

One Bad Man

INKLET #41

AMY LAURENS

www.inkprintpress.com

Print ISBN: 978-1-925825-32-9
eBook ISBN: 9781393476337

www.inkprintpress.com

National Library of Australia Cataloguing-in-Publication Data
Laurens, Amy 1985 –
One Bad Man
48 p.
ISBN: 978-1-925825-32-9
Inkprint Press, Canberra, Australia
1. Fiction—Fantasy—Dark Fantasy 2. Fiction—Short Stories 3. Fiction—Fantasy—Historical

First Print Edition: May 2020
Cover image © Irina Braga via Deposit Photos
Cover design © Inkprint Press
Interior art © Amy Laurens

ONE BAD MAN

IT IS COLD. THAT IS MY FIRST THOUGHT as I stand against the Bielgorod, the walls of the White Town, watching the Neglina River rush past in the dim, pre-morning light. Of course, October in Moscow is never what one might call tropical, but it has been many months since I was last up in the hours before dawn.

The frigid temperature numbs my nose, and the air, which in the heat would carry the scent of the river, smells of nothing but cold.

I draw my cloak closer around me

and hunker down into the gloomy shadows, waiting for one Vasiliy Ivanov to appear.

He will, at no later than two minutes past six, and I pull out my pocket watch—the bronze one with the roving green eye set in the lid, a token from Alexsey, my sponsor, and a not-so-subtle reminder that he is ever watching—and determine that I have but three minutes left to wait at most.

My breath puffs out, a misty white miasma in front of me, and my mind wanders back to the Chernye Miazmy, the black miasma that presently infect the town.

Hovering clouds of foul, dank darkness, they are spreading, quicker than before, and for all that they are careful to maintain face in public, I know that the administration is concerned.

Three deaths in three days would leave any governor anxious, and although the century is old, it is not so old that Moscow has forgotten the Plague—fifteen years ago and more than half my own lifespan, and yet as real as the warmth of my breath on my hand when I remember the faces of my parents as they died.

Thankfully, Gospodin Vasiliy Ivanov appears around the corner before I can fall further into reminisces. Fifteen years ought to be time enough to put away the memory of my parents' faces; alack, some days it is not.

But Ivanov draws closer, and I swallow down the bitterness that the memories dredge up, then detach the little gears-and-rods contraption that cuffs my right ear; I don't plan to let him out of my sight, so I should not need the hearing enhancement that the earcuff provides, and I do not want to risk it getting broken.

Alexsey would not approve of that.

So I slip the earcuff into a pocket hidden in the seam of my sarafan's skirts, exchanging it for another cuff that this time fits over the tip of my finger. I glance down, twisting it so the nib, similar to a quill but fashioned from bronze metal, sits over my nail. If I had a pot of ink at hand, I might write thusly; but this nib is not designed to hold ink. Instead, a tiny well is concealed in the band of the cuff. I apply light pressure to it, testing its hold.

Ivanov draws close and for a moment I hold my breath. If he spots me lurking in the shadows, I will have to forfeit today and come back again tomorrow—and that is assuming that he does not look close enough to learn my face.

But my mission is blessed—I cast a grateful glance skywards—and Ivanov passes me, entering the city centre through the iron gate that breaches the smooth white walls.

I fall into step behind him, my footsteps kept light on the grey gravel path so the rushing of the tributary can muffle them.

My pulse pounds as we tread through the murky pre-dawn in the White Town, and sweat begins to warm me under my arms even as the cold nips at my cheekbones, my chin, the tip of my nose.

Above, the stars are diminishing and light touches the eastern sky. I chew the inside of my lip and run my thumb nervously over the cuff on my finger, hidden deep in the folds of my cloak's warm pockets; logic tells me I should act now, while I can still be certain of both darkness and the element of surprise.

But I have to be sure.

Alexsey would be proud. The very notion of wanting to make *sure* that I am doing the right thing means that some small part of me questions my orders, and that means questioning the Order that disseminates them, which in turn means questioning the One who orders.

Alexsey is an atheist; he approves of questioning. I am a Shard; I am supposed to follow my orders.

My orders—God-given, monastery-ordained—have never been wrong yet, but a man's life is not a thing to trifle with, and so before I send Gospodin Vasiliy Ivanov, who has a wife and a mother and a dog and friends, from this life, I must make certain; I must *see* that he is a bad man.

That is why, as he pauses in the doorway of an old building whose paint is flaking and brickwork is crumbling and which carries the smell of rotted garbage and old fish, I do not seize the opportunity to lunge at him.

That is why, as he glances around, failing to see me, and enters the building through a rickety, wooden door, calling out a greeting to others inside, I do not give up and go home.

Others pose a problem, but not so large a problem as murdering an innocent man.

I hesitate by the doorway, uncertain. Should I enter, and risk making myself seen, or should I stay back, and risk losing my quarry?

A scream echoes in the building, cut short but nonetheless answering my question.

I adjust my hood over my head and ease open the door.

The scraping and thumps of a scuffle come from the right, so I take a deep breath and run.

It's been too long since I did this last.

Not the running; that I do regularly.

No, it is the adrenalin that my body is not accustomed to, the way nerves thrill through my stomach and my blood rushes past my ears. I know that afterwards it will leave me with a high that is very nearly addictive, but for now, the stress is greater than the excitement. At the end of this corridor, I will kill a man.

If I can make it there without losing the contents of my stomach, I add to myself; despite my regular practise, I am panting a little, and old fish and garbage and stale urine make me want to vomit.

Another cry rings out as I reach the splintered door at end of the hallway. I fling the door open and it crashes against the wall, making the occupants of the room flinch mid-stride.

There, that one is Vasiliy, with his dark great-coat flapping around him like bat wings, silver pistol a giant claw in his hand. He swings towards me, pistol raised, and I lunge towards him under the barrel of the gun.

As I dive, movement blurs to my right and I tackle Vasiliy, swinging him around to block me from whoever else is in the room.

I land heavily on my hip and just have time to register the fact that I'll have a spectacular bruise there tomorrow before Vasiliy is drawn down on top of me.

I look up over his shoulder at a young woman, hovering a few paces away with a bruise over her left cheek that could be the twin of my forthcoming one.

The strap of her sarafan is torn and her blouse ripped loose. Her eyes are wide. But before anyone else can act, I wrap my arm around Vasiliy's neck.

He struggles, but I draw the nib on my finger across the skin of his neck, pressing firmly. The well inside the cuff compresses against my fingertip, squirting poison like ink down inside the nib, which pierces his skin and delivers death into his veins.

He kicks against me and I push him away, kicking in my skirts to untangle my feet and right myself.

I am not worried about my soul any longer; this building has long been rumoured to be a centre for slave traffic and if I had any doubts, the fact that the woman can do no more than gnash her teeth at me from where her chains bind her in the centre of the room is confirmation enough.

It seems Gospodin Ivanov was indeed a bad man. And now—I glance at him dismissively—he is a dead man.

"Who are you?" the woman—probably not more than a girl, now I look again—asks of me.

I smile. "I am a Shard."

Her dark eyes widen in her pale face, and she shrinks back a little, gaze darting nervously to the body on the floor that once was called Vasiliy. "Oh."

I shrug and move towards her, flapping out my heavy skirts as I tuck the now-empty poison nib away. "He was a bad man."

"Yes." She bites her lip, twisting her fingers subconsciously in her sarafan. "Yes, he was."

I shrug again and gesture to the chains around her ankles. "The key?"

She glances up at me, then back to Vasiliy. "Around his neck."

I sigh deeply. Killing when my God commands it is something I do because it is necessary. Touching the dead, however, I much prefer to avoid.

Nonetheless, there are others in this building and if I am to get the woman out unharmed—or at least, without further harm—I must move quickly.

I kneel beside Gospodin Ivanov and swallow hard, praying for forgiveness as I prepare to desecrate the dead.

The smell of stale urine is thicker in here, even in the cold air. I suspect that, were I to stay in this room for too long, my eyes would begin to tear at it. As it is, I simply take a deep breath, and peel back the bad man's clothing, layer by layer, until I find the key on a chain around his neck. The clasp is stuck fast, but the chain just fits over his head, if I don't mind squashing his nose.

I grimace at the way his nose grows blotchy; with blood flowing in his veins no longer, the marks I have left with the key's chain may likely be permanent.

Footsteps slap in the hallway. I throw the key at the woman— "Here, hurry," —and press myself against the wall by the door.

As expected, the woman hunches over immediately to loose her chains— right in the centre of the room, in plain sight from the hall.

"Hey!" a man shouts. He is near: ten, fifteen steps at most. I stiffen. "Hey, stop, girl!"

Five, four, three…

I raise Vasiliy's silver pistol.

Two.

One.

A man in dark clothing bursts into the room, head hidden by a furred ushanka. He lunges at the woman, who is scrabbling frantically at the last lock.

I lunge at him, catching him in the back of the neck with a blow from the butt of the pistol that knocks him out.

He slumps, landing awkwardly across the woman's leg.

She shakes him off and hugs herself, trembling. "Dead?" she whispers.

I shake my head. "I had orders only for one," I say, stooping to unlatch the final clasp of her chains.

I take her hand and encourage her to step away. "Come," I say. "You are safe."

I have fulfilled my duty as a Shard; there is one less bad man in the world.

THE MAKING OF
ONE BAD MAN

If you've read Inklet #17, *Alone*, you'll have heard a bit of the story of *Jesscapades*, a novel I wrote way back when about an assassin-in-training and what basically amounts to discovering corruption in your religion.

Well. *Jesscapades* was the second novel I ever wrote, and while there is so much of it that's just sheer, unadulterated joy and delight, it's also a hot mess. I finished it, and realised I had about three or four different books going on in one.

It needed detangling. Badly.

Over the years, I tried out many, many iterations of the story, trying to get it to work. I'd list out all the cool bits of the original that I wanted to keep, sort them into piles of like-minded ideas, and go again from there.

I'm pretty sure that, instead of helping, all these attempts at detangling actually made things, much, much worse, at least in as much as I now have not one, but a whole suite of novels wanting to be written that are all entirely separate stories, but which kind of revolve around the same theme.

One Bad Man is one such attempt. This was a version of *Jesscapades* where the Shards were a secret subset of a literal religious order—and it was set in Moscow in the late 1700s, and there were maps and religious factions based on real events where different monasteries allied with each other to fight off invaders, and there was a dash of steampunk in there, and just… yeah.

Wow.

There was even a sub-version of this historical-Russian-steampunkishmonasteries version that was a choose-your-own-story version.

I'm not sure if I'll ever get around to actually processing all the research I did for this iteration of the Shards concept and writing it; and I think that if I did ever write it, now it would have basically nothing to do with the original *Jesscapades* concept except for 'female assassin'.

But either way, this little fragment has survived, giving you just the tiniest glimpse into the life of this fabulous Russian heroine that came to life in the chaos of editing *Jesscapades*.

DOWNLOAD YOUR FREE EBOOK

When you buy a print book from Inkprint Press, we like to say THANK YOU by offering you the ebook for free!

Please head to www.inkprintpress.com/inklets/41/ and the use the coupon INK41 to get your copy of this Inklet in epub AND mobi today!
(Coupon will only work once.)

HOW NOT TO
ACQUIRE A CASTLE

CHAPTER ONE

ON A HARD PLASTIC CHAIR IN THE FRONT row of the Great Hall in the world's fifth-best evil overlording academy, with its red-wooden parquetry floor that spoke of wealth and the beige, square panels of sound-boards speaking of conservatism on the walls, Mercury sat, pointedly not sweating.

Partly, this was because the Academy Administrators had deigned to turn on the air-conditioning earlier in the day, in recognition of the fact that the hall would be packed out with approximately six hundred bodies, all here to celebrate the graduation of about a third of that crowd.

But mostly, Mercury was pointedly not sweating because she made it a point never to sweat, sweat being an indication that she was working hard, and hard work being antithetical to her way of life.

However. If she *had* been sweating right now, it would not have been due to the uncomfortable warmth of six hundred packed bodies that even the air-conditioning system couldn't completely shift, or, in fact, from overexertion. Instead, it would have been caused by an even more unfamiliar concept in Mercury's emotional vocabulary: nervousness.

Mercury did not *get* nervous. Mercury got things *done*.

So the fact that she was sitting here, in the front row of the Great Hall, about to graduate from Evil Overlording Academy (with distinction), and was feeling *nervous*... She crumpled the black paper program in her pale fists. It made her furious, that's what it did.

Abjectly furious, that snooty-tooty Deviran with his stupid morals and his stupid I-don't-want-to-be-here and his stupid Overlords-are-empty-figureheads and his stupid face sitting ten people over, looking implacable with his deep brown skin and barely-there, precision-groomed beard, as though he knew it gave him a stupid air of alluringly stupid mystery…

Mercury scowled and searched for the train of thought that had been derailed, yet again, by Deviran's stupidity.

Ah. Yes. She was angry because she was nervous because she wasn't absolutely entirely one hundred and fifty percent sure that she'd beaten Deviran in their final exams, and 1) being anything less than a hundred and fifty percent certain of anything made her cranky, and 2) being beaten by Deviran for dux of the year would be utterly unbearable. She flicked away a piece of fluff that had become snagged under her immaculately magenta-painted nails and smoothed out the black paper program.

In the front corner of the hall, the starkly-attired string quartet with their traditional black instruments began playing the March of the Oncoming Doom. The screechy scrapes of hundreds of chairs on the hall's wooden floor sounded as the crowd climbed to its collective feet.

Mercury sat with her arms firmly folded for a few moments longer, until her best friend Sparky kicked her in the ankle.

"Get up, idiot," Sparky hissed, hints of real flame flickering through her flame-coloured pixie cut.

"No," Mercury said, flouncing to her feet and tossing her own glossy brown hair back over her shoulders. Four years she'd been playing by the Academy's rules in order to get what she wanted, and she'd had just about enough. Other people's rules should only be applied to plebs too stupid to invent their own.

Sparky rolled her eyes somewhere over Mercury's head before focusing on the stage, where the ceremonial party had begun entering.

Mercury clenched her jaw and narrowed her own eyes as the teachers of the Evil Overlording Academy filed onto the stage, dressed in their formal finery. Each teacher had their own distinctive look that matched their personality and their Overlording style, from severe charcoal suits to jet-black leathers, pastel ball-gowns and gem-toned lingerie and eye-blinding spandex, and even on one tiny old woman at the back, worn jeans and a grey flannel shirt. She was the one to watch out for, of course; Mercury could respect an Overlord who was confident enough in their abilities that they didn't need to telegraph them. It wasn't a look *she* would consider, of course, but still. She could respect it.

The band's march finished and, after a moderately awkward pause, the crowd sat. The Principal, pale skin and dark hair matching his suspiciously vampiric red-and-black suit, took the podium, and Mercury narrowed her eyes. He was doing a superb job of hiding his emotions—he was a premier Evil Overlord, after all—but she was Mercury, and unlike anyone else, she had the benefit of being able to rummage through people's consciousnesses. She was better at adding things *into* people's minds than taking information out, but he was telegraphing fear loudly enough that she could sense it without trying overly much.

Mercury pursed her lips.

Hmm.

The Principal cleared his throat at the blackened-wood podium, and the fear made it into his usually-unreadable eyes. "Before we begin," he said, and Mercury's stomach did a peculiar kind of flip-flop. "I have a pressing announcement to make regarding the safety of our students and their families."

He cleared his throat again and took out a sheet of paper from his pocket, unfolding it carefully and smoothing out the creases before beginning again. "The Council"—quiet booing echoed around the hall, and Mercury tsked impatiently—"have asked me to recommend that students from Tumul Tuos seriously consider postponing their return to town for a few days. The city is dealing with a *situation* at present which may present a danger to our students' health and safety."

Mercury's hands fisted at her sides and she forced herself to remain seated. What was wrong with her city? What had the Council mucked up now? A risk to the students' safety? There had to be more he wasn't telling them. Gently, Mercury tugged on his consciousness, implanting the suggestion that it might be better to share the news than to keep it secret. After all, how could they fight an enemy they didn't know?

"There are, ah…" He trailed off, glancing side to side as though wondering why his mouth had decided to continue.

Mercury didn't snicker, but she did press her lips together in satisfaction.

The Principal took a deep, steadying breath and seemed to change tack. "There has been one death already. The family have already been notified, so it is with much regret that I must inform you that Woovermyer will no longer be with us at the Evil Overlording Academy."

Murmurs broke out around the room, not all of them sad—to be expected in a school devoted to raising the next generation of dictators (ish) and despots (of sorts).

Mercury, however, crushed her program in her left hand, fist so tight her nails bit her palm.

"You okay?" Sparky murmured, leaning towards her.

Mercury gave a single, tense shake of her head and stared at the podium. Dead. Livie Woovermyer was dead in *her city*. And the Council hadn't done anything to stop it. Couldn't do anything to stop it, probably, given they'd warned the students to stay away. Livie hadn't been the strongest candidate in the year level, but she was no lightweight, either. It would take a lot of power to kill a Seven.

Enough was enough. A good thing Mercury was about to graduate at the top of the class, giving her the right to knock the lowest ranking current Overlord off their perch. Tumul Tuos would be hers in a matter of hours. And then there'd be no more of these wasteful deaths. Her city would be safe at last.

Madame Pompadour was up the front now, elbow gloves the same glimmery silver colour as her elaborate, piled-curls wig, eyelids gleaming with matching silver eye shadow, and abruptly Mercury realised Madame was there to make the announcement that would change her life forever. She leaned forward in her seat, ready to stand when her name was called.

"And now the announcement you've all been dying for," the Political Alliances teacher trilled, the frills on her evening gown fluttering as she moved. "The dux of this year's cohort!"

Sweat slicked Mercury's palms. Irritated, she reached over and wiped them on Sparky's thigh.

Sparky pushed Mercury's hands back into her own personal space bubble and Mercury, nervous to the edge of distraction, let her.

"Will you please join me in welcoming to the stage, our wonderful dux for this year, Deviran Goodsmith!"

Mercury froze halfway to standing. "Did she just say Deviran?" she whispered furiously to Sparky.

Sparky hauled her forcibly back down into her seat. "Yes," she hissed back. "Sit down, you're making a fool of yourself."

Mercury's spine snapped upright as she sat, and she arranged the folds of her long black skirt demurely. "No I'm not." She closed her eyes. "Deviran's going up to the stage, isn't he?" Even at a whisper, the misery in her voice was clear, but this time, she didn't care.

Sparky reached over and squeezed her hand.

Mercury squeezed back, lacing her fingers through Sparky's, and held tight as all her plans and dreams vanished in front of her.

A stone had landed in her chest. That must be it. Some strange sort of magic that made her chest contract and sink, and made the world distort for just a moment, long enough to trick her into thinking Deviran had beaten her so that someone could jump in front of her and yell SURPRISE!

Any moment now.

Any moment.

She refused to open her eyes and watch Deviran parading across the stupid stage like some stupid stupid-person, receiving his stupid medal and stupid symbolic crest pin.

It was that last exam question. She'd known Deviran would pull out his ridiculous 'Evil Overlords are merely figureheads, the Business Guild is where the power really lies' rant that everyone had heard a million times back when he was younger and angrier, and she'd tried to counter it, she really had.

She'd argued for the importance of the Overlording position, for the power of having a symbolic figure to unite the population in their hatred, for having a person able to make all the difficult, necessary decisions the Council was too weak and spineless to make... But it hadn't been enough. Everything she'd worked for, everything she'd set out to prove—and it wasn't enough.

There were words, there were names, and then forever later, once she'd died twice already, Sparky elbowed her in the ribs. "Come on," Sparky muttered. "We're up next."

And sure enough, there was a shuffling of presenters as the last of the Powers Behind The Thone graduates departed the stage, and the next speaker announced in threatening, funereal tones, "The Overlording cohort."

Mercury blinked furiously and followed Sparky to the end of the line at the right side of the stage. The other candidates proceeded one at a time across the stage, two girls and then stupid Deviran, and then a handful more and then Sparky, and then the speaker was calling her name.

Hands fisted, Mercury tossed her head high, climbed the four steps, and marched across the stage. She wouldn't look at them, the stupid faculty who'd denied her the city she rightfully deserved, and she wouldn't look the other way either, at the classmates and crowd undoubtedly sniggering at her failure.

She shook hands with the presenter, and while he pinned the tiny crossed-swords badge on her collar, her eyes betrayed her and slid towards the audience. Her stomach flipped as she saw the crowd of parents and friends behind the rows of students, all the way to the back of the hall, twenty rows at least, illuminated by the late afternoon light streaming in through the ceiling-high windows to the right. Everyone had someone here to watch them graduate. Everyone except Weird Al—and her.

The presenter finished with her pin, muttered something to her, and offered his hand again. Mercury coldly ignored it and strode from the stage. It didn't matter. None of it mattered. Tumul Tuos was her city anyway, and no one could change that. She'd think of something. She'd take a day or two out, make some plans...

And she could always hope that Deviran would choose some other Overlording territory. He'd be stupid to, but then again, he was stupid, so. Mercury could hope.

All at once, mid-way down the steps off the stage, Mercury came to rigid attention, scanning the room. Somewhere out there in the crowd, an exchange of power had just taken place, and it felt... unusual.

But the final few students were backing up behind her and muttering, so Mercury headed back toward her seat, craning her head all the while and searching for some sign of whatever it was that had just discharged a dizzyingly quiet amount of power into the room.

She sat, and Sparky leaned over. "Okay?"

"Mm," said Mercury. "Did you feel…" She accidentally caught the eye of the student behind her and twisted back to face the front.

"Feel what?"

Mercury turned it over in her mind. It had felt like a large shot of power discharged very quietly—but perhaps it hadn't been. Perhaps it had only been a small discharge after all, something most people wouldn't have noticed.

But still, something about it had tugged on her. It very nearly felt like something she'd felt before, only she *knew* she'd never sensed that kind of discharge before.

She shook her head. "Never mind. Don't worry."

Sparky sighed and straightened. "It's fine, Mercury," she said, drily exasperated.

"I know you didn't win, but I promise, you'll live through it."

Mercury waved a hand for silence.

The power had just discharged again, and it had come from somewhere in the back corner, far away from the windows and light.

Impatiently, Mercury waited for the formalities to conclude. The crowd stood while the quartet played the exit march, and the stage party left, Mercury tapping her foot all the while.

The moment the last notes of the march died away, Mercury turned and headed to the back corner, weaving in and out of the students and parents who had seemed to explode slowly but inexorably out from the neat rows of seating, ignoring Sparky's calls behind her. Power, something that tugged in a way that was strange and familiar, all at once. She pushed her way through a family posing for pictures—and halted.

In the shadows of the back corner, Deviran stood with his family, with his stupid, smug little smile, looking as tall and dark and stupidly alluring as ever. Prat.

His mother, short but sleek, and his father—tall, and utterly terrifying in a way not at all diminished by his gleaming smile—gushed over him, patting his back and hugging him tight. Within moments the Principal was there, glibly shaking hands and congratulating them on the success of their son. Something flickered across his consciousness, and also Deviran's father's—some moment of recognition in response to what they were saying.

But Mercury brushed it aside just as the mother brushed melodramatic tears from her cheeks and handed Deviran a silver-wrapped package about as long as her hand but half the width.

That. That was the source of the strange, magical feeling. Mercury watched hawk-eyed as Deviran unwrapped the gift. A glimpse of gold set her pulse racing—What was it? What did it do? Could she steal it?—and then the paper fell away to the floor, and Deviran stood staring wordlessly at the object in his hands, and Mercury did too.

Wide-eyed, Deviran raised his gaze to his parents, and even from where she stood Mercury could hear the reverence in his voice as he thanked them.

But Mercury had eyes only for the object. No wonder she'd felt it discharge, and no wonder it had felt both strange and familiar. In Deviran's hands lay a glorious, sunshine-gold key, large and strong—and with a handle in the shape of a stylised fish, long, flowing fins curving to make the grip.

A Key. They'd given him a Key. And not just any Key, but *the* Key, *her* Key, the Artefact of Power belonging to *her* city.

A wordless noise of wanting rose in Mercury's throat. Who cared about being dux? She needed that Key.

Keep reading! Head to
www.amylaurens.com/books/kaditeos
/castle
to buy your copy now!

ABOUT THE AUTHOR

AMY LAURENS is an Australian author of fantasy fiction for all ages. She does so many things that honestly, it's likely half of them are cover for a secret life as a spy, but who's to know.

Amy has also written the portal-fantasy *Sanctuary* series about Edge, a 13-year-old girl forced to move to a small country town because of witness protection (the first book is *Where Shadows Rise*), the humorous fantasy *Kaditeos* series, following newly graduated Evil Overlord Mercury as she attempts to acquire a castle, the young adult *Storm Foxes* series about magic and mental health, as well as a whole host of non-fiction.

See www.amylaurens.com for more.

INKLETS

Collect them all! Released on the 1st and 15th of each month.

Welcome to Dark Dale
LIANA BROOKS

When War Came to Town
A Powers Story
AMY LAURENS

Not Fantasy
AMY LAURENS

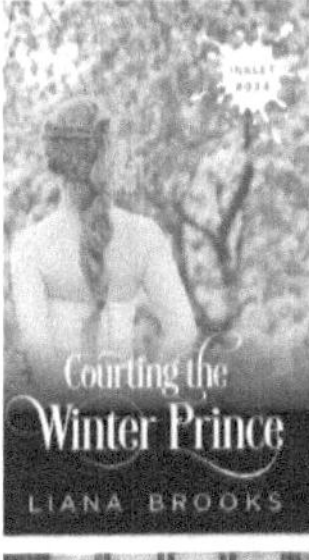

Courting the Winter Prince
LIANA BROOKS

At the Home of the Winter King
A Storm Foxes Story
AMY LAURENS

With This Ring
AMY LAURENS

Venus &
Seven Reasons I Said No
LIANA BROOKS

OATH KEEPER
AMY LAURENS

FORGET
A Powers Story
AMY LAURENS

INKLET #040
NOT QUITE
Cinderella
LIANA BROOKS

INKLET #061
ONE BAD MAN
AMY LAURENS

DOUBLE ISSUE
INKLET #042
The Claustrophobia
Of Loneliness &
Adam, Be A Star
AMY LAURENS

INKLET #043
The Artist
as a Young Girl
LIANA BROOKS

INKLET #064
CONFESSIONS
AMY LAURENS

INKLET #045
But For Snow
A Kaditeos Story
AMY LAURENS

INKLET #046
The Boy
Named NO
LIANA BROOKS

INKLET #047
Anamata
AMY LAURENS

INKLET #049
A Wolf FOR
Christmas
AMY LAURENS